PLIGHT OF THE GARGOYLES

Laura Shenton

PLIGHT OF THE GARGOYLES

Laura Shenton

Iridescent Toad Publishing

Iridescent Toad Publishing.

First edition. ISBN: 978-1-913779-89-4

Prologue

The sun cast a warm, golden hue over the quaint medieval village, where gargoyles lived in harmony. Their homes, made of timber with thatched roofs, blended seamlessly into the surrounding landscape. Poverty was no stranger to them, yet they were rich in happiness and camaraderie. The nearby woods provided game for hunting, while the market held every so often served as a gathering place to exchange goods and stories.

In the dusty streets, young Strymar played blissfully with her gargoyle friends, their emerald skin and wings shimmering in the sunlight. They clutched dolls resembling baby gargoyles, giggling and chattering amongst themselves just as any group of young children would.

"Look! Mine can fly higher than yours!" Strymar exclaimed.

She vibrantly tossed her doll into the air and then caught it in her thin arms.

"Ah, but mine can do flips," her friend retorted, imitating the motion with his own doll.

Their laughter chimed through the quiet streets, reflecting the sense of peace and unity that had long thrived in their community.

"Hey, do you think we'll be great hunters someday?" one of the other young gargoyles asked, her eyes wide with innocence and hope.

"Of course we will!" Strymar replied, puffing out her chest with determination. "We'll catch chickens, and boars, and deer. We'll bring them back to the village and make everyone proud!"

As the young gargoyles played, Strymar's thoughts turned to her parents, wondering what they would think of her aspirations. She knew they wanted only the best for her, just as all the adults in the village looked out for one another. For now though, she was content to live in the moment, blissfully unaware of the challenges that lay ahead.

As she continued to play, the sun dipped lower

in the sky, casting long shadows across the cobblestone streets. The sound of laughter and friendship filled the air, a testament to the resilience and spirit of the gargoyle community.

Suddenly, a shrill cry pierced the air. Strymar's heart lurched as she saw a mother gargoyle, her eyes wide with terror, sprinting towards them.

"Hide!" she urged, her voice strained with fright. "The humans are coming! I spotted the Opal Faction heading in this direction on my flight back from the market. They're too close for comfort!"

The children froze, their blood running cold at the mention of the dreaded Opal Faction. Strymar's mind raced, trying to make sense of the situation. She had heard stories about the humans, how they hunted and imprisoned gargoyles. But why would they come here?

"Inside, now!" barked Strymar's father, suddenly appearing in front of her.

He scooped her up in his strong arms, the fear in his eyes betraying his usually calm demeanour. Strymar clung to him, searching for reassurance.

"Da… Dad, what's going on?" she stammered, her voice barely audible over the mounting turmoil.

"Nothing you need to worry about, sweetheart," he said, forcing a smile that didn't quite reach his eyes. "We just need to get inside, alright?"

As her father hurried her into their home, Strymar could feel her chest constricting with each panicked breath. Her thoughts whirled like a tornado as she tried to comprehend the impending danger. Why were the humans attacking? What did they want? And what would happen to her family and friends?

"Mum!" Strymar called out, seeking solace in her mother's embrace.

There was no response.

"Where's Mum?" she asked her father.

"Your mother is helping others find shelter," he replied, his voice tense. "She'll be ok, Strymar. Just stay here with me."

Strymar's world felt like it was crumbling around her. The peaceful village she had known and loved was now shrouded in alarm and uncertainty. She bit down on her lower lip, trying to hold back the tears that threatened to fall.

"I'm scared, Dad," she whispered, gripping his leg tightly.

As they huddled together in their home, danger loomed closer. They had no time to think ahead when the deafening clash of weapons and guttural battle cries filled the air. The Opal Faction had arrived and they were storming through the village.

Strymar peered through a crack in the shuttered window, her heart pounding wildly in her chest. The humans were ruthless, slaughtering her fellow gargoyles without hesitation or mercy.

"Get away from the window," her father said quickly, protectively trying to pull her back.

But Strymar couldn't tear her eyes away from the commotion outside. She watched in horror as the invaders tore through the surrounding homes, looting anything of value and setting fire to everything else.

"We can't stay here!" her father said frantically.

Their own home had now succumbed to the relentless embrace of flames. In their unforgiving hunger, the embers danced with malevolence, casting eerie shadows that flickered on the very walls that had once stood as the family's fortress.

"Don't let them find you!" her father shouted before running outside and disappearing into the pandemonium.

Strymar hesitated for a moment, and then darted out after him.

"Mum! Dad!" she cried out, dodging the snarling flames that licked at her heels.

She frenziedly scanned the crowd for any sign of her parents. The air thickened with acrid smoke, a sombre shroud that hung heavy in the wake of the fiery onslaught.

"Mum! Dad!" Strymar shouted, her voice trembling as tears streamed down her face.

Realising that she had no idea where her parents could be amongst the chaos, panic gripped Strymar's throat like a vice. She had to find them, no matter what.

Strymar ran further into the destruction. She looked up to see gargoyle corpses falling from the sky, struck down by arrows fired with deadly precision from the humans' bows. It was clear that attempting to fly above the fray wouldn't save her or advance her search for her parents. Despite this, she saw that even those attempting to escape on foot were being hunted mercilessly.

"Please, where are you?" she sobbed, choking on the smoke that filled her lungs.

Just as she turned another corner, the strong arms of a human soldier encircled her, dragging her backwards. She struggled in vain against the iron grip, her small gargoyle frame no match for the man's brute strength.

"Let me go!" she screamed.

Her pleas fell upon deaf ears as her captor shoved her into a fortified wooden cart alongside other terrified gargoyles. The cramped conditions made it impossible to sit or stand comfortably. Everyone inside was forced to huddle together, wings pinned uselessly to their sides.

"Has anyone seen my mum and dad?" Strymar

cried out, desperation lacing her voice.

An elderly female gargoyle looked at Strymar with a mixture of pity and fear, wanting to offer comfort but unable to find the words.

"Shh, child," she whispered softly. "We must stay quiet."

The caged gargoyles murmured amongst themselves, some arguing about the lack of space while others tried to console one another. Then, a wiser gargoyle spoke up, his gravelly voice barely audible above the din outside.

"We are being taken somewhere terrible," he warned. "There is no guarantee we will survive."

Strymar clung to the cold bars of the cage, her disappointment heavy and her mind racing. As the cart began to move, she could only watch as thick plumes of black smoke billowed into the sky, leaving the once-peaceful village in a pile of ash.

As the human army marched proudly alongside the horse-drawn cart, their duty was clear: to guard and escort the caged gargoyles to their destination. Strymar stared at the soldiers through the bars, her sense of dread mingling with a growing anger. These humans had invaded her peaceful village and torn everything apart.

The journey seemed to stretch on forever, with the unforgiving sun beating down on the captive gargoyles. Their throats were parched, and they longed for even a single drop of water to quench their thirst.

One brave gargoyle dared to call out to the guards, his voice raspy and weak.

"Water... please, we need water..."

Without warning, a cruel guard reached through the bars of the cage, grabbing the gargoyle's claws that poked out in their compromised position. In a violent grip, he squeezed tightly, and with a sickening crunch, broke every bone below the gargoyle's wrist. The injured gargoyle stifled a scream, tears streaming down his face.

"Silence!" the guard barked, glaring at the rest of the gargoyles. "Not another word from any of you!"

The message was clear: if they didn't keep quiet, things would only get worse. Strymar clenched her fists, her discomfort increasing as she tried to suppress her own cries for help. She couldn't let these humans break her spirit, but she also knew she needed to be careful.

After what felt like an eternity of jostling along uneven terrain, the creaking cart ground to a halt outside an ominous structure that loomed menacingly. The harsh stone walls stood like silent sentinels, their imposing stature casting a foreboding shadow over the weary gargoyles. The air itself seemed to carry the weight of captivity, thick with the remnants of countless tales of despair that must have unfolded within the unyielding fortress.

As the occupants of the cart gazed up at the high-security bastion, they took in the cold, unforgiving form of fortified towers and iron-clad gates. Each brick, each rusted hinge, seemed to tell a story of hellish confinement. The very architecture spoke of an indomitable will to restrain.

A guard then opened the cage.

"Move!" he shouted, prodding the gargoyles with a sharp stick as they stumbled out onto the hard ground.

Strymar's wings ached from having been pinned for so long, and her legs felt weak and unsteady. But she knew that now was not the time to falter. It was clear to her that she was about to be imprisoned in the most awful of conditions.

18

Chapter One

Carried by a determination born from years of imprisonment, Strymar stumbled through the dense undergrowth, gasping for breath as she forced her aching limbs to keep moving. The woods were thick with shadows, the gnarled trunks of ancient trees twisting and looming in the darkness. Moonlight filtered through the canopy overhead, casting eerie silver beams onto the dusty ground.

The relentless growls and snarls of the hounds resonated through the bleak landscape as they pursued Strymar, their fetid breath hot on her heels. With every ounce of strength she had left, she pushed herself to run faster, ignoring the pain that coursed through her weary body.

She winced with each step as her wounds screamed in protest. Blood seeped from the gashes on her arms and legs, staining her pine-coloured skin a deep crimson. Her body glistened with sweat, and her wings hung limply at her sides, too damaged to carry her aloft.

Can't stop, she thought, gritting her teeth. *Have to keep moving. Have to survive.*

As she sprinted, her mind flashed back to a memory she wished she could forget.

"Keep your eyes open, gargoyle scum!" one of the prison guards had barked at her, jabbing a metal pole into the ribs of a fellow prisoner who had dared to divert his gaze from the gruesome scene unfolding before them. "Remember what happens when you try to escape," another prison guard had said whilst motioning to the male gargoyle in the centre of the courtyard. The poor soul had attempted to flee the confines of the Opal Faction's prison, only to be dragged back by the vicious hounds. Along with a group of randomly selected prisoners, Strymar had been forced to line up against a wall and watch as the hounds ravenously tore at their victim's chest. With her eyes locked onto the grisly sight, the screams of the dying gargoyle had churned in her ears, mixing with the sadistic laughter of the human guards.

Strymar frantically shook her head in a

desperate attempt to rid herself of just one of the many cruel memories she'd acquired during her years of captivity. A cold knot formed in the pit of her stomach, her hatred for her captors and the fear of suffering the same fate battling for dominance within her.

She couldn't bear the thought of being humiliated and tortured; she would find freedom or die trying.

The baying of the hounds grew louder, their frenzied howls echoing through the dark woods. Strymar's heart raced as she pushed herself to run faster. Every step persisted to send jolts of pain through her wounded body, but fighting against the agony, she refused to let it slow her down.

Damn those beasts.

The gruesome memory of the fellow prisoner's botched escape attempt refused to leave the corners of her mind. She had watched so helplessly as the hounds had tore into his flesh, their bloodlust insatiable. The laughter of the human guards still lurked in her thoughts, a stark reminder of their cruel nature.

Keep running, damn it, she told herself, her

resolve hardening. *You've come too far to give up now.*

As she sprinted through the abundant foliage, her thoughts turned to the other prisoners she had left behind. Were they thinking about her now, wondering if she would make it? Did they dare to hope for their own freedom, or had they resigned themselves to a life of captivity and misery?

The howls of the hounds grew louder still, and Strymar's chest tightened with fear. She tried to focus, but her thoughts were a whirlwind of panic. She darted left, then right, trying to throw the hounds off her trail. But they were unyielding, their predatory snarling closing in on her like an ever-tightening noose. The sound filled her ears, drowning out everything else.

Feeling the first tendrils of defeat creep into her mind, she couldn't help but cry out in exasperation. She was desperate for something, *anything*, to show her the way.

As if in answer, the ground beneath her suddenly gave way as a twig snapped viciously around her feet, sending her sprawling face-first onto the hard earth. Grit and leaves filled her mouth as she frenziedly tried to push herself back up, but a sudden jolt of pain tore through her ankle, forcing a scream from her lips.

Panic bubbled in her throat as she registered that a hound had clamped its jaw onto her. She frantically clawed at the ground in a futile attempt to escape the beast's iron grip. She knew that even if she somehow survived this, there would be no mercy waiting for her back at the prison. She would be facing not just torture and humiliation, but death.

"Get off!" she said, her voice thick with anger.

She just about managed to land a weak kick on the hound's snout with her free leg, but the animal held firm, its growls mingling with her cries of suffering.

Suddenly, the air was filled with a cacophony of yelps and howls, a symphony of agony and rage that quivered through the trees. Strymar felt the smallest glimpse of relief to notice that no longer was her ankle hostage to the vice of a canine grip.

Confused, she lay still, struggling to comprehend what was happening. Giving her no opportunity to gather her thoughts though, a shadow fell over her. Instinctively, she looked up. Her gaze was met by the cold eyes of a human hunter, tall and imposing.

"I see you've caused a great deal of trouble for the Opal Faction, haven't you?" he said with a sneer as he drew a wickedly curved knife from his belt. "They're clearly not up to the task of keeping you in check."

"Who the hell are you?" Strymar demanded bitterly, her breath still coming in ragged gasps.

"Someone who's going to make sure you never cause trouble again," he answered, his tone icy and detached. "I'm with the Inner Circle, and you're our prisoner now."

Like hell I am, she thought, fury rising within her like bile.

But fear kept her silent, and she could only watch helplessly as the hunter advanced closer towards her, his knife gleaming in the moonlight.

"Your defiance is admirable," he continued, a cruel smile twisting his lips, "but utterly pointless. You're mine now, gargoyle."

Strymar's mind raced, searching for an escape, scrambling for a way to turn the tables on the hunter. She knew that for every second she stayed on the ground, injured and vulnerable, her chance of freedom was slipping further from her grasp.

She snarled, defiance surging through her veins like wildfire. She couldn't let this man – this Inner Circle hunter – rob her of everything she had fought so damn hard for.

"Over my dead body!" she roared.

Using the last reserves of her strength, she pushed herself to her feet and sprinted further into the woods, ignoring the searing pain in her wounded ankle. Branches whipped at her face, but she didn't care; all that mattered was escape.

Chapter Two

Finally, Strymar burst into a moonlit clearing. She felt like she had been running for hours, but it was hard to tell how much time had passed. She had no way of knowing how far she had come, or how close she was to safety.

Having spent years in captivity, the sight of the twinkling stars overhead took her breath away. They shone brightly above her, as if beckoning her to look up and embrace the expanse of the night sky. She greedily drank in the beauty of the celestial bodies, filling her soul with a desperate hope that all was not lost.

The air was heavy with the sharp smell of pine, and the chorus of crickets filled the night with a gentle, comforting sound. She could feel the soft grass of the clearing beneath her feet, but still the moment was too fragile for her to ignore the reality of her situation.

She stared at the lake before her. The vast expanse of water was a daunting sight. It seemed to stretch out into the ether. Despite the minimised state of her wings, she knew that she would have to fly over it in order to be certain that nobody from the woods could catch up with her. The agony of her injuries was still fresh, and the thought of flying over such a large body of water filled her with dread, but she knew it was her only chance.

I just need to fly.

Her wings, tattered and unused for so long, protested as she unfurled them. Every initial beat sent fresh jolts of pain coursing through her, a cruel reminder of the wing torture she'd had to endure in prison. With no choice though, she let out a guttural cry as she launched herself into the air. She began to soar over the deep lake, tears streaming down her face as she fought against the white-hot agony.

I must keep going. I've come too far to give up now.

With her wings slicing defiantly through the cool air, Strymar relied on her acute sense of smell for guidance: if she was to have any chance of survival, she would need to seek out other gargoyles.

She knew what she was looking for: in the clandestine realms beneath the earth's surface, lived gargoyles who had managed to avoid being captured by the humans. They had carved out a subterranean existence, concealed from prying eyes and persecution. Dwelling in hidden communities, their underground lairs served as sanctuaries, offering refuge.

Strymar's flight over the lake took her beyond the water and into the woods, until finally, her senses led her to a small, unassuming entrance nestled within the gnarled and ivy-coated trunk of an enormous tree.

As she gazed hopefully at the entrance, the strain of her arduous flight lingered in the sinews of her wings, a testament to everything she'd had to suffer in pursuit of sanctuary. Yet, despite the ache that taunted her entire form, a palpable relief washed over her as she recognised the familiar scent that wafted from within; the essence of her kind was unmistakable.

Bunching up her weary wings and tired blood-stained body, she summoned the last vestiges of strength, and with unwavering determination, crossed the threshold into the concealed refuge. Under the weight of her exhaustion, not only did she seek respite for her fatigued body, but also solace for her restless soul.

Scaling down the hollow insides of the ancient tree trunk, Strymar descended into the bowels of the earth, navigating through the crooked roots that intertwined with nature's subterranean tapestry. The air thickened with an earthy musk as she continued her descent, the twisted bark beneath her claws telling tales of centuries past. The dim glow of luminescent fungi illuminated her path, guiding her through the intricate maze of roots until at last, she reached the level ground of the concealed gargoyle lair. The transition to the underground depths marked not only a physical descent, but a symbolic arrival into the hidden heart of gargoyle kinship.

Attempting to get her bearings, Strymar felt a chill creep over her. She could barely see a thing, but she sensed the labyrinthine tunnels stretching out around her, the damp earth walls pressing in on all sides. Anxiety clawed at her chest, but she forced herself to continue forward, driven by the burning desire to survive.

Stumbling through the gloom, she reached out a trembling arm to steady herself against the cold stone walls that now surrounded her. The air was heavy with not just the musty scent of being underground, but other gargoyles. She clung to it like a lifeline as she pressed on.

Praying that every turn would bring her closer to her goal, she couldn't help but notice an increase in her anxiety, gnawing at her resolve. She growled through clenched teeth, forcing the despair from her mind. She couldn't afford to lose hope now. Not after everything she'd suffered.

At last, after what had felt like hours of agonising travel, Strymar stumbled upon two gargoyle guards standing watch over a large chamber. Relief flooded her body, followed closely by a renewed sense of purpose. She had made it. But now, she needed to prove herself to these gatekeepers, to show them she was worthy of joining their ranks.

"Please," she said, her voice hoarse with exhaustion and desperation. "I need your help."

"Who are you?" one of the guards demanded, his voice echoing in the cavernous labyrinth.

Strymar was all too aware that she was a pitiful sight to behold, her skin stained with blood and dirt, and her wings trembling from their almost unbearable exertion.

"I'm Strymar," she replied, barely managing to keep her voice steady. "I've escaped from the Opal Faction's prison. I need to speak to your leader. Please, I mean you no harm."

The guards exchanged wary glances, but seemed to sense the authenticity in her tone.

"Very well," said the taller guard. "We'll take you to Grydovyn. But be warned, any sign of treachery will be met with swift consequences."

"Understood," Strymar agreed, relief washing over her at the prospect of finally finding sanctuary.

Chapter Three

As the two guards led Strymar deeper into the labyrinth, she marvelled at the intricate network of tunnels and chambers that had been carved into the earth. The walls shone with a faint luminescent glow, casting jagged shadows on the rough stone surfaces. The air was damp and cool, a stark contrast to the oppressive atmosphere of the prison she had left behind.

Still though, the journey to the main hall was both awe-inspiring and nerve-wracking for Strymar. She couldn't help but wonder what kind of reception awaited her. Would the leader believe her story? Would he see her as a threat, or as an ally?

When they finally arrived at the main hall, Strymar could hardly believe her eyes. It was a vast underground chamber, reminiscent of a grand old church sanctuary. With towering columns sculpted from stone, it was adorned with elaborate carvings of gargoyle history. Intricate frescoes decorated the ceiling; their colours muted by the low lighting, yet still vibrant, they depicted scenes of ancient battles and heroic deeds.

"Behold," said one of the guards, gesturing proudly at their surroundings, "the heart of our civilisation."

"It's amazing," Strymar whispered, her awe momentarily overshadowing her anxiety.

"Come," the taller guard urged, leading her towards the throne.

At the far end of the hall, a magnificent stone throne sat upon a raised dais, flanked by statues of other gargoyles. As Strymar was led onwards, a figure rose from the seat, his powerful wings unfurling behind him. He was an imposing presence, with piercing eyes that seemed to bore into Strymar's very soul.

"Welcome, stranger," he spoke, his voice deep and resonant. "I am Grydovyn, leader of this underground sanctuary. What brings you before me?"

"Thank you for seeing me, Grydovyn," Strymar

began, mustering all of her courage. "I'm Strymar. As I told your guards, I have escaped from the Opal Faction's prison. My journey has been long and dangerous, but I had to reach you – not only to ask for shelter, but to tell you what I know."

Grydovyn studied her intently, weighing her words.

"Tell me, Strymar," he said, his eyes never leaving hers. "What have you endured? What is it that you must share with us?"

Strymar swallowed hard, feeling the memory of her experiences threatening to crush her.

"I... I've been imprisoned by the Opal Faction for most of my life. They treat us like animals, torture us, and force us to live in fear."

Grydovyn's expression darkened, but he remained silent, encouraging Strymar with a nod of his head.

"During my escape," she continued, "I discovered something that could change everything for us. The humans... they're not as united as we thought. There are divisions among them."

"Divisions?" Grydovyn asked, leaning forward. "Explain."

"Before I managed to get away," said Strymar, "I encountered a human who claimed to be from a different society called the Inner Circle. He wasn't part of the Opal Faction, but he still wanted to capture me. It seems they have their own goals and conflicts."

"Interesting," Grydovyn mused, stroking his long chin. "This is new information indeed. If there are fractures among the humans, perhaps we can exploit these divides to our advantage."

Strymar nodded, her heart racing. She knew sharing this information was critical, but she couldn't help but worry about the consequences. Would this revelation lead to greater conflict, or a chance at freedom for gargoylekind?

"Thank you, Strymar," Grydovyn said, his voice firm but kind. "Your bravery and resourcefulness are commendable. We will discuss this further and determine the best course of action."

Strymar felt a mixture of pride and trepidation. Not only had she risked everything to escape the prison, but she had stumbled upon vital information that now rested in the possession of a gargoyle leader. It was now up to him to decide what to do with it.

Whatever comes next, she told herself, *I will face it head-on.*

Grydovyn graciously nodded his head, and then fixed his steely gaze on the two guards standing to attention before him.

"Ensure Strymar receives proper medical care and a quiet place to rest," he ordered, his voice bouncing off the cavernous walls.

The guards saluted in unison and moved to carry out their leader's command.

As Strymar was led away, she breathed a sigh of relief, feeling a glimmer of hope for the first time in ages. Perhaps here, among her own kind, she would find the strength to not only heal, but to fight for the freedom of others.

Chapter Four

The next day, the grand underground hall buzzed with anticipation as hundreds of gargoyles gathered to hear Grydovyn's address. Their wings rustled like whispers in the shadows as they settled into every available space.

"Silence!" Grydovyn commanded, causing the murmurs in the hall to cease instantly as he stood tall on a raised platform to look out over the sea of expectant faces. "My fellow gargoyles, I have called you all here today because we now have a particularly brave soul among us – Strymar."

Grydovyn recounted Strymar's harrowing escape from human-enforced captivity. The crowd listened intently, hanging on his every word as the gravity of the situation sank in.

"Until now," Grydovyn continued, "we believed the human threat to be unified, a single force seeking our subjugation. But whilst on the run, Strymar's discovery has revealed that there are two divisions of humans above ground: the Opal Faction and the Inner Circle. For all we know, the Inner Circle could simply be one of many groups who exist and function separately of the Opal Faction."

A hushed murmur swept through the gathered assembly, reverberating against the stone walls as the revelation hung in the air. Expressions of shock and surprise were aplenty as everyone grappled with the astonishing notion that the humans, often perceived as an indomitable force of disdain, were not a united front. Whispers of disbelief and realisation intertwined, forging a shared understanding amongst the gargoyles that, perhaps, the threads of human enmity were more fractured than they had dared to believe.

"The question before us is whether we can use this division to our advantage," Grydovyn stipulated, his voice rising with fervour. "Can we take on the humans in a war and reclaim our right to live without fear at ground level, to hunt freely and bask in the daylight?"

Private conversations rippled through the crowd as gargoyles weighed the potential risks and rewards. Some spoke with zeal about the possibility of freedom, while others expressed concern about the casualties that would inevitably result from such a conflict.

"Enough!" Grydovyn bellowed, silencing the chatter once more. "I understand your concerns, and I share them. Any decision will not be made lightly, I promise you."

"We trust you, Grydovyn," a voice rang out from the gathered gargoyles, strong and impassioned. "You've always led us wisely!"

Grydovyn nodded solemnly, his eyes sweeping over the sea of faces, their fates resting on his shoulders. The weight of their trust bore down on him, but he knew it was his duty to make the best decision for them all.

"Thank you," he said humbly, acknowledging the gargoyle who had spoken up, and then addressing the crowd. "I will carefully consider our options and consult with our council. Together, we will determine the path forward."

As the meeting adjourned, Grydovyn watched the gargoyles disperse – some with hope shining in their eyes, others with worry furrowing their brows. He knew that whatever he decided, there could be no such thing as the perfect outcome. For the sake of his kind, he vowed to choose the path that offered the greatest chance of prosperity.

"May the winds guide us," he whispered, steeling himself for the challenges ahead.

Chapter Five

Over the next few days, Grydovyn found himself pacing the dimly lit corridors of the underground labyrinth, his mind racing with thoughts of war and peace. The stability of everyone's future rested heavily on his shoulders, their whispers repeating in his ears as he brooded over strategy and tactics, risks and rewards.

As a wise leader, Grydovyn knew that he couldn't make such a monumental decision on his own, and so, just as he had promised, he summoned his council – a select group of esteemed gargoyle advisors – to discuss the matter of concern. They gathered around the expanse of a stone table in the heart of the labyrinth, their hushed voices blending with the distant drip of water from the cavern walls.

"We stand at a crossroads," Grydovyn began, his voice steady and resolute. "The knowledge that the humans are divided has opened a door for us, but we must decide if we are willing to step through it and face what lies beyond."

The council members exchanged glances, their expressions a mixture of concern and determination. They too understood the gravity of the situation, and the potential consequences of their actions.

"Let us weigh our options carefully," Grydovyn said, encouraging an open dialogue among the council.

The council of gargoyles conversed, their voices rising and falling like the rhythm of a distant storm. As they debated, Grydovyn listened intently to their insights, his eyes narrowing in thought.

"We cannot remain hidden forever," declared one gargoyle, his voice brimming with a deep resonance. "The humans persist in their persecution. We must defend our kind."

A murmur of agreement rippled through the assembly, yet dissent lingered in the hesitant gazes of some.

"To wage war risks exposure," argued a more cautious voice. "Our survival has always depended on secrecy. I miss living above ground just as much as the next gargoyle, but should we really run the risk of losing everything: our home, our family, our friends?"

The debate continued to echo through the subterranean chamber, the council grappling with the conflicting options that could shape the fate of both gargoyle and human alike.

It was then that Frydon, a younger and more ambitious member of the council, seized the opportunity to make his move. Sensing Grydovyn's hesitation to wage war, he leaned forward and spoke with a dominance that commanded the room, his fiery gaze locked on the leader.

"Are we to cower here in the shadows while the humans continue to trample on our rights?" Frydon challenged, his voice dripping with disdain. "Is that the legacy you wish to leave behind, Grydovyn?"

Another murmur pooled through the council, some nodding in agreement whilst others frowned at Frydon's accusatory tone. Grydovyn recognised the undercurrent of resentment in Frydon's words, and his jaw clenched as he suppressed a flare of anger.

"Every decision I make is for the betterment of our community," Grydovyn replied coolly, meeting Frydon's fiery gaze with steely persistence. "I will not lead us blindly into a conflict that may cost more than it gains."

Frydon sneered, his eyes glinting with bitter ambition.

"Then perhaps it's time for a change of leadership," he retorted, an attempt to goad Grydovyn further. "Perhaps someone with more courage should take the reins."

The council members gasped, their eyes widening at the audacity of Frydon's challenge. Such a contest had not occurred within the community for quite some time. The tension in the room was palpable.

Grydovyn stared at Frydon, his heart pounding, but his features betraying nothing but calm determination. He knew that to refuse a leadership challenge would show weakness, and to fight was to honour tradition and maintain order within the ranks.

"Very well, Frydon," Grydovyn replied, his voice committed and unwavering. "If it is a challenge you desire, then it is a challenge you shall have.

We will settle this matter according to our ancient customs."

Frydon smirked, clearly satisfied with the turn of events.

With a regal nod and an air of quiet dignity, Grydovyn acknowledged the challenge as a prelude to destiny. A subtle undercurrent of purpose emerged from deep within. His participation in the challenge wouldn't merely be a defence of personal authority; it would be to fight for a style of leadership born of wisdom and empathy, not ego and arrogance.

Chapter Six

The cavernous expanse thrummed with hushed conversation. Flickering candle flames cast dark patterns upon the stony walls. The towering ceiling would allow for flight during the impending battle, a crucial aspect of any gargoyle fight.

On the ground in the centre of the vast space, a large circle had been drawn with the menstrual blood of a female gargoyle. Not only was it to mark a boundary not to be crossed by spectators, but to symbolise life, beauty, and pain.

An anxious tension weaved its way through the crowd of gathered gargoyles. Attendance was compulsory for all – even the youngest among them. Every gargoyle needed to understand the magnitude of challenging a leader. Wings twitched and claws tapped on the ground as everyone awaited the arrival of the combatants – Grydovyn and Frydon.

"Last time I saw a challenge like this, there was blood everywhere," an older gargoyle whispered to his companion. "I remember it like it was yesterday. Brutal, it was."

"I hope Grydovyn wins," a younger gargoyle muttered nervously, his eyes darting around the chamber. "He's always been a fair leader, and I don't trust Frydon."

"True, but Frydon might have a point about not stalling when it comes to waging war on the humans," another chimed in, his voice laced with worry. "We've been hiding down here for so long now."

The murmurs ceased abruptly as Grydovyn stepped into the circle, his muscular form bathed in the subtle glow from the candles. He stood stoically, his gaze focused and unyielding. A few members of the crowd shouted words of encouragement, but he paid them no mind; his thoughts were consumed by the battle ahead.

"Go get him, Grydovyn! Show them who's boss!" yelled a particularly enthusiastic gargoyle from the sidelines.

"Crush that arrogant bastard!" another added.

Grydovyn's controlled expression never wavered as he coolly scanned the crowd. He knew every gargoyle before him could rely on his wisdom and steady leadership to keep them safe in this treacherous world. As long as he drew breath, he would not let them down.

Right on cue, Frydon entered the arena with a dramatic flourish, his wings outstretched and his chest puffed up. He grinned maniacally at the assembled gargoyles, clearly relishing the attention. The wiser members of the community exchanged disapproving glances – it was clear to them that Frydon was underestimating the seriousness of the situation.

"Ready for the show, ladies and gents?" Frydon coaxed with a smirk, flexing his claws. "I promise I won't make it too painful to watch."

"Such arrogance," a gargoyle grumbled nearby, eliciting nods of agreement from those around him.

"Remember, Frydon, this is no mere performance," Grydovyn warned, his voice deep and measured. "It's a battle to the death."

"Of course," Frydon replied, snorting and

flicking his tail dismissively. "I've been waiting for this moment for a long time, old gargoyle."

"Then let us begin," Grydovyn said solemnly, unfurling his wings and preparing for battle.

"Finally!" Frydon said with a sneer, his arrogance dripping from every syllable. "You must be eager to die, Grydovyn."

Immediately, Frydon lunged forward, claws outstretched. Grydovyn nimbly dodged the attack, his wings flaring for balance. The crowd held their collective breath as the two combatants circled each other within the blood-marked boundary. This was it: the moment of truth that would determine the fate of their underground domain.

"Predictable as ever, Frydon," Grydovyn mused, his expression unreadable. "Your impatience will be your undoing."

"You underestimate me," Frydon said, spitting on the ground in disdain.

Frydon launched himself into the air and swooped down with a vicious slash of his claws. Grydovyn ascended in response, narrowly avoiding contact. He analysed every move, every feint, searching for weaknesses to exploit. He knew he couldn't afford to make a single mistake.

The clash of wings and claws reverberated throughout the cavern, the duel an intricate dance of skill and strategy. In a whirlwind of movement, the two gargoyles charged at each other in flight, their wings slicing through the air with a rhythmic cadence.

As the battle raged on, every spectator felt the ebb and flow of tension in each sweep of motion. In the midst of the arduous conflict, time became a fluid concept. The very space seemed to hold its breath as the opponents became all the more embroiled in what was beginning to feel like an eternal struggle.

"Is that all you've got?" Frydon taunted from above, a wicked grin on his face.

Refusing to take the bait, Grydovyn charged stealthily at Frydon, their nimble bodies colliding in midair with a resounding crack. The force of the impact sent them both plummeting downwards.

"Come on, Grydovyn! You can do this!" a young gargoyle shouted from the sidelines, her voice wavering with fear and hope.

As they spiralled towards the ground, Grydovyn could feel Frydon's strength beginning to wane. The younger gargoyle had fought without strategy, wasting energy on flashy moves meant to impress rather than subdue. Grydovyn had conserved his own strength, waiting for the perfect moment to strike.

Bruised, bloody, and battered, Frydon fought on, the determination in his eyes struggling to mask the toll the battle had exacted. His diminishing strength was evident. His claws were torn, and his wings, once held high in defiance, now faltered with each strained beat. His attacks, once fierce, now carried the weight of hopelessness.

With each attempted strike, Frydon's movements grew slower, more laboured. The once-proud gargoyle continued to falter under his injuries, the agony etched across his impassioned features. Yet, despite the defeat written in the language of his wounds, he pressed on with a tenacity that bordered on being reckless.

Grydovyn, though wearied, was resolute, an

enduring pillar against Frydon's relentless onslaught. Despite his exhaustion, he parried Frydon's advances with an almost ethereal grace. Many in the crowd had never doubted him, but it was still a shocking sight to behold.

In the final throes of the struggle, as Grydovyn skilfully evaded Frydon's weakened strikes, it became clear that the once-audacious challenger was now fighting not against his leader, but against the inevitable.

Frydon snarled, attempting one last desperate attack as once again, the pair hurtled towards the unforgiving stone floor. Seizing his opportunity, with a powerful shove, Grydovyn sent Frydon careening off course, causing him to smash into the ground with a sickening crunch.

The cavern fell silent, save for the ragged breaths of the combatants and the distant drip of water from the ceiling above. Grydovyn landed gracefully in the circle, his wings outstretched like a victorious guardian angel. Frydon lay crumpled and bloodied nearby, gasping for air and struggling to rise.

"Your arrogance has been your downfall, Frydon," Grydovyn stated, a note of pity in his voice. "You don't have what it takes to be a leader."

All around him, the crowd murmured in agreement, their conversations tinged with relief and admiration. They knew Grydovyn had proven himself worthy as a leader, not just through strength, but through strategy and wisdom. As their voices swelled, hope spread through the gathered gargoyles – war or no war with the humans, the future of their underground domain would at least have a better chance of survival under Grydovyn's leadership.

Meanwhile, Frydon fought to stay conscious amidst the pain that wracked his body. Every breath drawn was a testament to the ebbing flame within him, a flicker that fought against the encroaching darkness. The crowd muttered in hushed tones, their expressions a mixture of pity and curiosity.

"Please," he said, wheezing, his trembling claws reaching out for help that he knew would not come. "Don't... let me die like this."

As if in answer to his plea, a blood-curdling scream pierced the air. A female gargoyle burst from the crowd, her eyes wild with panic and fear as she sprinted towards him. Shock rippled through the gathered onlookers, who had never expected anyone to care so deeply for the notoriously promiscuous and callous Frydon.

"Get back!" shouted a burly gargoyle, lunging forward to intercept her. "You can't enter the circle before it's over!"

She couldn't be stopped. With tears streaming down her face, she threw herself at Frydon's side.

"Frydon!" she cried out, her voice cracking as she cradled his head in her lap. "No, no, it can't be! I don't want you to die."

The cavern fell silent, all eyes fixed on the tragic scene unfolding before them. Even Grydovyn seemed taken aback by the revelation, his weary gaze lingering on the grieving female for a moment longer than necessary.

As Frydon's shallow breaths diminished, the cavern walls seemed to groan a lament for the fallen challenger. The perishing gargoyle, now succumbing to his demise, faced the inevitable passage from one life to the next.

With a deep sigh, Grydovyn turned to his

guards and gave the command.

"Remove Frydon's body," he said solemnly, "and clean this space."

The guards hesitated, glancing between their leader and the sobbing female clutching at Frydon's now lifeless form. However, Grydovyn's expression brooked no argument. Reluctantly, they stepped forward, gently prying the distraught gargoyle away from her lover's corpse.

"Forgive me," Grydovyn said under his breath, his eyes downcast.

As he watched the guards carry Frydon's body away, Grydovyn knew that it was the only way to uphold gargoyle tradition and maintain order. Equally though, as the female's anguished wails echoed through the cavern, he couldn't help but feel a twinge of guilt for the hurt he had caused.

Mortified, Strymar pushed her way through the crowd, her emerald wings folding protectively around her as she approached the bereaved female.

"Hey," she said gently, softly touching the poor

gargoyle's shoulder. "I know this must be hard for you, but you can't stay here. Let me aid you in finding refuge."

The female looked up at Strymar through tear-flooded eyes, her breath hitching as she tried to regain composure.

"Who are you?" she asked cautiously.

"I'm Strymar. I didn't know Frydon well, but I don't want to see anyone hurting like this. Come with me, please."

"Ok," the gargoyle conceded, nodding numbly. "I'm Carriemyre."

Dazed from the shock of it all, Carriemyre allowed herself to be led away from the grim scene. Strymar guided her through the labyrinthine passages, eventually bringing them to a small alcove tucked away in a quiet corner. The two gargoyles settled down on a moss-covered ledge, illuminated by only a few candles.

"Talk to me," said Strymar, breaking the silence.

"Everyone thinks Frydon was a bastard, and

they're not wrong," Carriemyre admitted, her voice trembling. "He hit me, forced himself on me, and made me feel worthless compared to his other lovers. But I still cared about him."

"Oh."

"You're new here, Strymar, but I'm sure it won't be long before you think of me as stupid. Everyone else does."

"I don't think you're stupid," Strymar replied sincerely, shaking her head with empathy. "You're kind, sensitive, and deserving of so much more than what he gave you. You're allowed to care, and you're allowed to *grieve*, even if others don't understand."

"Thank you," Carriemyre whispered, her eyes glistening with gratitude. "What about you? Why did you come to help me?"

"Seeing you in pain reminded me of my time as a prisoner under the humans," Strymar confessed. "I couldn't comfort those who were suffering without risking further wrath, punishment, torture – you name it, the prison officers did it. I know what it's like to feel alone and afraid."

As the two female gargoyles sat in the aftermath of loss, a glint of shared understanding was evident between them – a subtle affirmation that, even in the darkest moments, camaraderie endured.

Chapter Seven

Strymar lay on her bed, her viridian wings folded beneath her as she stared at the surrounding soft embers. The flicker of candlelight cast dancing shadows across the rough-hewn walls of the dark little alcove she had been allocated. It was a modest space, nestled deep within the labyrinth. It served as her sanctuary in this underground world. The bed, a simple slab of rock adorned with a few tattered blankets and furs, provided minimal comfort, but served its purpose well enough. A small wooden table held the meagre belongings she'd been given upon her arrival: a cracked ceramic bowl, an ancient-looking book with dog-eared pages, and a small pile of firewood for those nights when the chill crept too close.

Despite its humble appearance, the alcove had a certain cosy charm, symptomatic of how all gargoyles underground had to make do with what little resources had been scavenged from above ground. It was a reminder that even in the depths of their subterranean refuge, life persisted against all odds.

Strymar's thoughts drifted back to the brutal battle between Grydovyn and Frydon, replaying each gruesome blow in vivid detail. Blood had splattered across the stone floor, and the air had been thick with the scent of iron and death.

"Damn it, Frydon," she muttered under her breath.

Although the duel had been agreed upon by both participants, watching the bloodshed unfold had left a bitter taste in her mouth. It reminded her all too much of the horrors she'd witnessed while imprisoned by the humans.

She recalled the cruel laughter of the Opal Faction guards as they had tortured her fellow gargoyles, the screams of pain undulating through the dank cells. The memory sent shivers down her spine, even as the candlelight offered some semblance of warmth.

What's the difference? she wondered, angry and frustrated. *In the end, it's all just death and suffering.*

She clenched her fists, her claws biting into her scaled palms. She knew duels for leadership had always been part of community tradition, and she was fully aware that she couldn't erase the atrocities committed by the humans. All the same though, she couldn't help feeling that there must be a better way, a path beyond the seemingly endless cycle of violence.

She sighed heavily. For now, all she could do was to survive and adapt, as the gargoyles had always strived to do.

She closed her eyes, attempting to find solace. Just as she was about to slip into the realm of sleep, a faint but unmistakeable sob echoed through the alcove, jolting her awake.

Her eyes snapped open, and she saw Carriemyre standing at the entrance, tears streaming down her face. It was clear that Frydon's death weighed heavily on her, despite his unpleasant mentality and cruel treatment.

"Can I... Can I sleep in here tonight?" Carriemyre asked hesitantly, her voice wavering with emotion.

Strymar nodded, remembering all too well the crushing loneliness and lack of privacy she'd experienced during her years in prison.

"Of course," she said softly, making room for Carriemyre on the small bed. "Come on in."

Carriemyre crossed the cramped area, the flickering candlelight casting long shadows across her face. She sat down on the edge of the bed, her body trembling with suppressed sobs.

"Thank you," she whispered, wiping away her tears with the back of her bony wrist. "I just... I can't be alone right now."

With a subtle grace, Strymar extended one of her wings, a silent invitation for Carriemyre to settle down beside her. The simple yet comforting gesture spoke of kindness and understanding. Carriemyre, appreciating the unspoken invitation, laid down, the cool stone beneath her offering a stark contrast to the warmth of shared companionship. She nestled in close to Strymar, finding a haven in the winged embrace.

"I know he was a bastard to me, but I still cared about him, you know? And now he's gone..."

Carriemyre burst into a fresh wave of tears. Each acrid drop, a poignant testimony to her loss, traced down her cheeks and pooled on the frigid stone beneath. Strymar, ever vigilant in her silent support, felt the sorrowful tremble of Carriemyre's form.

"Let it all out," Strymar soothed, feeling a sense of empathy and responsibility for Carriemyre's pain. "You don't have to pretend to be strong right now."

Eventually, Carriemyre's breathing began to gradually slow until her sobs subsided. Exhausted from the emotional turmoil, she drifted off to sleep, her body still trembling slightly.

As Strymar held Carriemyre close, she found herself struggling with a gnawing sense of guilt. The more she thought about it, the more she believed that if she hadn't informed Grydovyn about the divided humans, none of this would have happened. Perhaps Frydon would still be alive, and Carriemyre wouldn't be mourning him.

As much as Strymar tried to suppress her thoughts, they clawed at her mind, refusing to give her peace. Sleep, when it finally came, was restless and plagued by nightmares – visions of blood and death, screams from the prison cells, and the haunting question of whether everything was her fault.

Her mind churned with regret and dread. She knew the gargoyles needed a strong leader, especially if they were to face the humans in war. But how could she reconcile her actions in view of the consequences they'd brought?

Chapter Eight

Strymar's eyelids fluttered open, her sleep having been tumultuous and plagued by nightmares. Her mind raced as she untangled herself from Carriemyre's sombre embrace.

Strymar knew she needed to speak with Grydovyn about everything that weighed on her conscience – both for her own sake and for the future of the underground community. She urgently left the small alcove and padded softly through the dimly lit passages of the labyrinth, in search of the leader.

"Excuse me," she called out hesitantly to a passing gargoyle. "Could you point me in the direction of Grydovyn?"

"Down that way, take a left at the fork and head straight," the gargoyle replied with a friendly nod. "You'll find him in the healing chamber."

"Thank you," Strymar replied, heading off to follow the directions.

As she approached the small chamber, she could hear the murmurs of conversation between Grydovyn and two gargoyle assistants, who were tending to the injuries he'd acquired in battle against Frydon.

She took a deep breath. Steeling herself for the difficult talk ahead, she then entered the chamber.

Grydovyn looked up at her.

"Strymar, is everything alright?" he asked, concern etched on his features.

"May I talk to you about... everything?" she asked humbly.

"Of course," he said gently. "Please, take a seat."

As Grydovyn dismissed his assistants with a wave, Strymar nervously sat down on a raised slab of cold stone.

"I can't help but feel responsible for all that's happened," she said, her voice trembling. "If I hadn't told you about the humans being divided, maybe Frydon wouldn't have challenged you."

"Strymar," Grydovyn began, his tone a blend of compassion and firmness. "A good leader must be prepared to face the truth, no matter how difficult. If Frydon hadn't challenged me over this particular issue, he would have found another reason eventually. You can't blame yourself for his actions."

"Still," Strymar persisted, "I feel terrible knowing that my actions may have led to all this suffering."

She glanced away, her eyes brimming with unshed tears as she thought about Carriemyre and how much distress she was in.

"Listen," Grydovyn said, leaning forward, his voice soft but resolute. "There will always be individuals like Frydon who believe they have a divine right to lead out of arrogance and ego. What matters now, is what we do moving forward."

After a long pause, he shifted the focus of the conversation to the more pressing matter.

"I still haven't made a decision about whether

our underground community should go to war with the humans. I need to know more about what it's like for the gargoyles above ground under the human reign of terror."

Strymar swallowed hard, the memories of her time in captivity surging back like a tidal wave.

"There are no gargoyle villages left," she said hoarsely. "All gargoyles above ground are imprisoned by the humans."

"Tell me more about the prison you were in," Grydovyn urged gently, his eyes filled with a quiet determination. "I need to understand the extent of the suffering."

Strymar's breath hitched as she described the horrors she'd endured – the starvation, the torture, the deplorable living conditions, and the sadistic brutality of the guards. The words poured out of her in a torrent of anguish and fury, painting a harrowing picture of life above ground for the imprisoned gargoyles.

As Strymar recounted her experiences, Grydovyn listened with unwavering attention, his face a mask of muted resolve. He knew the decision he had to make would not be an easy one, but it was essential for the survival and future of their kind. Looking into Strymar's haunted eyes, he understood that the weight of such decision rested not only upon his shoulders, but on the hearts of every gargoyle in the community.

His focus never faltering as he took in the raw emotion on Strymar's face, Grydovyn could see how difficult it had been for her to recount the atrocities she'd witnessed and experienced above ground.

"Thank you for your candour, Strymar," he said solemnly. "I can see that this conversation has taken its toll on you. I promise to give your words the consideration they deserve as I weigh our options. They will help to inform my decision. No matter what, we are all in this together."

Strymar gave a small, appreciative nod, grateful for the understanding.

"Anyway," said Grydovyn, mindful of Strymar's wellbeing. "How are you holding up after your escape from the prison? You sustained quite a few injuries on your route to freedom."

"Ah, yes," Strymar replied, her gaze drifting to the healing wounds on her legs. "They're still sore, but they're mending much better than if I'd been captured by the Opal Faction and thrown back into that hellhole. I owe you my thanks for the food and the bed I've enjoyed since joining your community."

She looked up at Grydovyn, sincerity shining in her eyes.

"Living underground, we have to be resourceful, but we always strive to provide the best for everyone here," Grydovyn said with a hint of pride. "Even though we know it's not much compared to what we once had."

Strymar nodded her head in agreement, her expression earnest.

"It may not be like the days when gargoyles lived freely above ground, before the humans took over," she said, "but what you've given me here is miles better than anything I could have dared to hope for back in the prison."

Grydovyn knew he had much to contemplate. The knowledge of the human division presented an opportunity, but to risk the lives of all gargoyles in a war against their oppressors was not a decision he could take lightly.

Having spoken to Strymar, he was now acutely aware of the suffering endured by the gargoyles above ground in the prison – a suffering he desperately wanted to alleviate. But first, he needed to determine if waging war against the humans was truly the best course of action, particularly for the gargoyles underground who had worked so hard to build a life for themselves, no matter how humble.

As he mulled over his thoughts, Grydovyn couldn't help but feel the burden of his responsibility as a leader bearing down on him. And yet, he knew that he must rise to the challenge, guiding his community through this difficult time with wisdom, courage, and compassion.

Chapter Nine

In the dark corridors of the underground maze, Strymar moved with determination as she navigated through the winding passages. Her gaze flickered across the rough stone walls, searching for the chamber where Grydovyn might be found. The sound of her steps mingled with distant voices of her fellow gargoyles in other parts of the labyrinth.

When she finally found Grydovyn, he was alone in a small chamber, hunched over a small ceramic bowl of mealworms. She hesitated at the entrance, watching him consume the protein-rich food with gratitude, despite its simple nature. His calm demeanour and air of authority commanded respect, even in this humble setting.

"Ah, Strymar, join me, please," he said without looking up, his tone warm and welcoming.

Taking a seat on a cold stone slab, Strymar took

a deep breath, certain of what she wanted to say.

"Grydovyn, I've been thinking about the human from the Inner Circle," she began, her voice wavering slightly. "The one I encountered in the woods during my escape."

Grydovyn paused mid-bite, his gaze fixed on Strymar as he gestured for her to continue.

"Our encounter was brief, but intense," she said, the words now tumbling from her mouth. "He wanted to capture me, but I fought back with everything I had – anger, desperation, sheer and absolute willpower. But, Grydovyn, I've come to realise something: we don't really know anything about the humans of the Inner Circle."

"True," Grydovyn mused, his brow furrowing. "We know little of their intentions or capabilities."

"Exactly!" Strymar exclaimed, her voice growing stronger. "If we were to wage war against the humans and only face the Opal Faction in doing so, we'd have some idea of the enemy. But with the unknowns of the Inner Circle to consider, we could be walking into a minefield. We don't know what they do with captured gargoyles, how big their population is, or what their overall objective might be!"

Grydovyn leaned back, his expression thoughtful as he digested Strymar's words.

"You raise valid concerns," he said. "Our knowledge of the Inner Circle is indeed limited. You've brought up important points that we must consider."

As Grydovyn opened his mouth to consume another bite of his humble meal, a sudden cacophony of noise erupted from a nearby chamber. The sound was jarring, clearly indicating trouble. He and Strymar exchanged worried glances before moving to rush towards the disturbance.

Upon entering the large chamber, they were met with a chaotic scene – a full-blown brawl had erupted amongst the crowd. Gargoyles were throwing punches, claws were scraping against skin, and cries of pain filled the air.

As Strymar looked on in shock and bewilderment, Grydovyn clenched his jaw, his eyes narrowing as he surveyed the sight before him. It was more of a brutal skirmish than a deadly battle, but it was still astonishing all the same. The underground community had always been rooted in co-operation and camaraderie; this outbreak of casual violence was chronically out of character.

Grydovyn knew he needed to stop the fight without causing further harm or resentment. He urgently jumped up onto a tall stone plinth, and, taking a deep breath, bellowed out a commanding roar.

The sound rumbled through the chamber like thunder. The brawl began to slow as heads turned to face their leader.

"Enough!" Grydovyn shouted, his presence radiating authority.

The fighting then ceased entirely. The crowd stood in stunned silence, their attention fixed on Grydovyn. They couldn't help but admire the dignified way in which he had managed to regain control.

"Look at yourselves," Grydovyn said, his voice stern but tinged with disappointment. "This is not who we are!"

Shame clouded the faces of the brawlers as they

hung their heads, immediately regretting their actions.

"Speak, my fellow gargoyles," Grydovyn demanded of the ashamed crowd. "Tell me what led you to such disharmony."

"We were discussing whether we should wage war against the humans," a burly gargoyle called out, his bruised face a testament to the brawl. "Tempers flared, and then everything just escalated."

"Indeed," another added, his wings drooping with remorse. "Some of us believe that war is the only way to reclaim our freedom, but others fear the consequences and feel that the risk is too high."

"Let us not fall prey to infighting," Grydovyn urged, his voice softening. "We are gargoyles. We stand united. I understand your concerns. Each path holds its own risks, but I ask you this: Is tearing each other apart the solution? Are we not stooping to the level of those who have oppressed us for so long?"

The injured gargoyles looked at each other in apologetic silence as the weight of their leader's words settled upon them.

"Look around you," Grydovyn continued, his gaze sweeping across the pool of chastened faces. "We are one – united by the bonds of kinship and shared suffering. If we allow differences of opinion to divide us, then we are no better than the humans above ground. We must stand together if we are to overcome the challenges that lie ahead. United, we are strong; divided, we fall. Now, go and tend to your wounds. Reflect on what has transpired here today, and let it be a lesson for us all."

As the crowd dispersed, murmurs of agreement and reflection filled the air. Strymar approached Grydovyn, her eyes brimming with unshed tears.

"Please forgive me," she said. "I never meant for this to happen."

"Do not blame yourself, Strymar," Grydovyn replied, his tone firm and reassuring. "You are just as much a victim in this as any of us – perhaps all the more so."

As the last of the crowd left the chamber, Strymar felt a mixture of emotions wash over her. She knew the stakes were high, but with Grydovyn's wise, measured and dignified leadership, perhaps the gargoyles still had a fighting chance.

***

Later that day, Grydovyn stood in a quiet alcove within the furthest outskirts of the lair. Water dripped noisily into a small puddle on the ground, the irritating sound mirroring the turmoil within his thoughts. He could no longer deny the truth; the fractures among his kind were growing and something had to be done.

"Enough," he said, his voice low, passionate with conviction. "We must face our destiny."

Grydovyn emerged from the small alcove and into one of the many veins of the labyrinth, his every movement informed by a measured resolve. With a gaze that conveyed no room for discussion, he beckoned the first gargoyle he encountered.

"Everyone is to gather in the main chamber," he commanded, his voice cutting through the subterranean stillness like a clarion call. "Spread the word."

The gargoyle, sensing the urgency in Grydovyn's tone, didn't waste a moment.

Without hesitation, he darted away into the labyrinth's twists and turns.

Word spread like wildfire in the cool, musty air, igniting a palpable tension that coiled around the cavernous chambers. The anticipation hummed like a current, an electric charge that quickened the pulse of every gargoyle who caught wind of the impending gathering. Whispers, like fleeting shadows, danced along the walls, carrying the message that something significant was about to unfold.

In their eagerness to find out what was going on, the entire community was swift in their movement to the main chamber. The crowded space, now teeming with expectant gazes and hushed murmurs, became an environment of shared apprehension. The air seemed to thicken with significance, every gargoyle present aware that the forthcoming revelation would shape the trajectory of their hidden existence.

With a commanding presence that seemed to carve through the ambience, Grydovyn took his place upon the large stone plinth before the crowd. The whole cavern yielded to a hush as the collective gaze of the gargoyle community fixated on their leader.

"My fellow gargoyles," he announced with certainty. "It is time to unite and make a stand. In three days' time, we will go to war against the humans."

The cavern exploded into a cacophony of reactions – some gargoyles roared in approval, while others gasped in fear. Female gargoyles, their eyes wide with worry, protectively clutched their young. Some of the male gargoyles clenched their fists, claws digging into their palms in their eagerness to reclaim their rightful place above ground.

"Three days isn't enough time to get ready for something like this," one gargoyle fretted, his expression a picture of terror.

"Damn right it is," a burly male gargoyle retorted nearby, his voice laced with anger. "We've been waiting too long for this day. It's time to teach those humans a lesson they won't forget!"

Through all this, Strymar's emotions swirled like a tempest: guilt and dread mixed with righteous fury. She knew that some gargoyles would perish in a war, and part of her felt responsible. However, she also longed to see the Opal Faction pay for their cruelty, and for the gargoyle prisoners to be liberated.

"Silence!" Grydovyn shouted.

The clamour subsided as everyone turned their attention back to their leader.

"I understand your fears and your anger. We must face this challenge together. Years of hiding in the shadows has made us complacent," he insisted, his eyes ablaze with determination. "It is time for us to rise up, find the weaknesses of our enemies above ground, and exploit them to secure our future."

As the weight of Grydovyn's decision settled upon the crowd, many gargoyles wore expressions of stoic acceptance and unfettered belief – they knew they would follow their leader into the fray.

"Prepare yourselves," Grydovyn commanded, his voice resonating throughout the chamber. "In three days' time, we will fight as one – not only for our freedom, but for the future of our kind."

An odd mixture of dread and hope hung in the air. The decision had been made, and there was no turning back. War was coming.

Chapter Ten

The central chamber of the labyrinth hummed with anticipation. Each gargoyle's eyes gleamed with readiness, their wings twitching nervously behind them.

"Silence!" Grydovyn commanded, his voice booming through the space as he stood amongst the crowd.

The chatter instantly ceased, every eye turning to meet the leader's steely gaze.

"We stand here today at the precipice of change," he said. "We must be organised and strategic in our approach, for the humans, regardless of their allegiance, have deadly weapons. But do not forget: we possess strength, cunning, and a will forged in the fires of adversity. Let us use those qualities to our advantage. Train hard, hone your abilities, and never lose sight of our ultimate goal: freedom!"

Echoes of agreement reverberated through the chamber, the atmosphere seeming to pulse with a shared heartbeat.

"Today, we prepare for war. To lead us in this endeavour, I present to you our esteemed head of the war council, Drygor."

A hulking figure stepped forward from the shadows, his granite skin etched with healed battle scars that spoke volumes about his experience and prowess. His eyes burned with a fierce determination, yet there was something undeniably likable about him, a sense of camaraderie that drew others in.

"Some of you will know Drygor already," Grydovyn enthused. "As an esteemed member of our community, he has proven himself as someone who can be trusted to lead. Not only that, but Drygor was nothing short of excellent in protecting his village against the humans – prior to the collective decision compelling all gargoyles to seek refuge underground."

The air seemed to hum with a collective understanding that Drygor's expertise would serve as a cornerstone in navigating the challenges ahead. The assembled gargoyles, their features etched with respect, eagerly awaited the burly gargoyle's words. They stood poised to absorb the lessons and strategies that would shape their approach against the humans.

"Thank you, Grydovyn," said Drygor, his confident yet endearing voice carrying through the chamber like thunder. "I am honoured to stand before you all today. As your new trainer and commander, I promise to guide you towards victory, but know that such a feat will require discipline, willpower, and unyielding commitment! Under my command, you will become an unstoppable force! Together, we will face the enemy, save the imprisoned, and reclaim our place above ground!"

The expressions on the faces of the assembled gargoyles shifted. It was clear that Drygor's words resonated with them, igniting a spark of hope within that had been dormant for far too long.

"From this day forth," Drygor continued, his voice a mixture of steel and warmth, "we train as one. We fight as one. And by the gods, we will triumph as one!"

A chorus of roars and cheers erupted from the crowd, their forms shaking with fervour. Even the most sceptical among them couldn't deny the fire that coursed through their veins.

"Alright, everybody," Drygor barked, his voice commanding the space. "We need to be organised and efficient in our preparations. Divide yourselves based on your skills and expertise! Be honest with yourselves and with others when it comes to what you think you can offer. Don't doubt yourselves on the basis of inexperience. Today is about training. Today is about *learning*. If you're physically strong, we need you in combat. If you're a good flier, we need you in combat."

Gargoyles shuffled around, their wings brushing against one another as they found their places. Groups formed, each focused on different tasks: combat training, weapon forging, and strategic planning. The sound of claws scraping against stone was almost drowned out by hushed conversations and whispered plans.

"Hey, you!" Drygor called out to a muscular gargoyle lingering at the edge of the combat group. "What's your specialty?"

"Close-quarters fighting," he replied with confidence. "Used to do a lot of it back in the day."

"Join the frontlines," Drygor directed, pointing to a cluster of similarly built gargoyles.

As Drygor moved throughout the groups of gargoyles, assigning tasks and offering guidance, resolve grew stronger.

"Those humans won't know what hit them," he bellowed endearingly, his eyes flashing with defiance. "Together, we are stronger than they think. We've survived in the shadows, and now it's our time to rise up and reclaim our lives."

***

With every calculated strategy, every sharpened blade, and every practiced combat manoeuvre, the community grew more prepared for the upcoming conflict. The deafening clash of metal against metal rang through the cavern as gargoyles engaged in fierce combat training. Their skin glistened with sweat as they pushed themselves to their limits.

"Keep your guard up, Kryzak!" Drygor barked at a young gargoyle who had stumbled back from a particularly powerful strike. "You're not going to last five minutes against the Opal Faction if you let your defences down like that!"

"Got it, Drygor," Kryzak replied, panting and wiping the sweat from his brow as he repositioned himself for another round.

All around the training area, gargoyles wore committed expressions. They were fighters, survivors – willing to give their all in the campaign for freedom.

"Good work, everyone," Drygor called out assertively as he strode around the large chamber, pacing himself to allow for observation. "You're all getting stronger, faster, and deadlier. Keep pushing yourselves."

As duelling gargoyles continued their intense practice, Drygor moved to the weapon forging area, where the air was thick with the smell of molten metal and burning coal. The rhythmic pounding of hammers against anvils filled the space, accompanied by the occasional hiss and sizzle of red-hot iron being quenched in water.

"That's some fine craftsmanship," he said, running a claw along the edge of a newly forged blade. "This'll slice through the humans like butter."

"Thanks, Drygor," responded the gargoyle blacksmith, wiping the sweat from his brow with the back of his arm. "Your determination is driving us all to do our best."

"Keep up the good work," Drygor encouraged, turning his attention to another gargoyle who was carefully hammering heated metal into shape. "We're going to need every last weapon we can get."

"Understood," the gargoyle replied, not pausing in his diligent work.

As the gargoyles worked together, forging an arsenal that would be their key to victory, there was a swell of pride and conviction in the air. They were quickly becoming a force to be reckoned with.

"Remember what's at stake, everyone," Drygor said firmly as he continued his surveillance of the chamber. "Our freedom, our lives, our very existence; we won't let any human control or destroy us any longer. Together, we'll make them pay for everything they've done to us."

Chapter Eleven

The clang of metal striking metal chimed through the vast underground chamber as the gargoyles continued in their preparations for war. Sparks flew from the anvils where skilled artisans hammered out blades, their muscular arms rising and falling in a hypnotic rhythm. In another corner, warriors sparred, their speed and balance improving with each blow.

"Excellent!" Drygor bellowed as he weaved his way through the space, his features twisting into an encouraging grin. "That's it! Stay focused!"

He then turned his attention to a pair of sparring gargoyles.

"Plant your feet firmly on the ground, and use your tail for balance," he advised, demonstrating the stance. "And remember to keep your knees bent, so you can dodge or change direction quickly."

"Thanks," the younger gargoyle replied, his eyes glowing with gratitude as he adjusted his posture to attempt the stance. "It feels better already."

"Excellent," Drygor encouraged, clapping him on the shoulder before turning to move on. "Keep practicing."

From a quieter part of the chamber, Strymar watched the gargoyles in training, her wings folded around her like a protective cloak. She couldn't help but feel a mixture of awe and anxiety at the sight – the sheer force of a large community united in a common cause. Although she felt a spark of pride, it remained tainted with the sense of responsibility.

Seated in a circle with a group of wise, older gargoyles, she listened intently as they debated strategy. Their voices were measured and thoughtful, a stark contrast to the cacophony of battle that raged around them.

"Alright," Drygor said, approaching the group and addressing Strymar. "We need you to remember everything you can about your journey from the prison to here. Every detail could be crucial. We need to know what we're up against."

Strymar's mind raced back to the terrifying ordeal of her journey from the prison to the labyrinth. As the only gargoyle underground who had escaped human captivity recently, she knew her knowledge of the world above would be vital to the war effort.

"I'll do my best," she said, swallowing the lump in her throat. "But I was fleeing for my life, so some details might be blurred. I was panicking when I escaped, so there might be inaccuracies. And those damn hounds didn't make it easy. Also, you have to understand that I was just a young gargoyle when the Opal Faction captured me. The world outside is still so unfamiliar to me."

"Understood," Drygor replied gently, sensing her unease. "Just tell us what you can. Anything you can give us will be invaluable."

"Alright," Strymar began, taking a deep breath. "As soon as I was out of the prison, I was in a large, barren area – no houses, just carts and stables for the Opal Faction's horses. Then, not far from that, I entered a large wood. With all the tall trees and foliage, it would probably be the perfect place for an ambush if we could navigate the depths without getting lost."

"That's something we could work with," one of the strategists said, thoughtfully scratching his chin. "It could certainly be used to our advantage."

"Once I left the woods, I came to a clearing where I flew across a vast lake," Strymar continued, her voice growing more confident as she recounted her journey. "And after that, I just followed my instincts, really. That's how I found this lair."

"Thank you, Strymar," Drygor said, his voice warm with gratitude. "You've given us some excellent information to work with."

As the strategy team huddled closer together, an older female gargoyle began to sketch a rough map on the stone floor, using chalk to trace Strymar's harrowing journey. Drygor guided their efforts, his keen mind working tirelessly to formulate the best plan of attack.

"Considering the lack of human presence along the majority of Strymar's route," he mused aloud, "I think our best approach would be to ambush the prison. If we can catch the Opal

Faction off guard and prevent them from spreading word of our advance, it'll give us a significant edge."

To Strymar's surprise, the other strategists didn't hesitate to agree with the plan. Her heart pounded with a chaotic mixture of excitement and trepidation as she envisioned a powerful scene of every last prisoner breaking free from the oppressive grip of the Opal Faction. At the same time though, she couldn't shake the fear that the humans might be stronger. What if they captured or even killed the gargoyles in response to such a daring assault?

"Are you all sure about this?" Strymar asked, nervous, but keen to voice her concerns. "To underestimate the humans could be a fatal mistake."

Drygor's gaze met hers, his eyes burning with impassioned certainty.

"They won't know what's hit them," he declared. "Back in the days when they targeted our villages, they outnumbered us. This time, it will be different. This underground community exists because many different villages joined forces to build a life down here in this labyrinth. Against the Opal Faction, we shall no longer be outnumbered in battle."

As Strymar looked around the vast chamber, she saw the truth in Drygor's words. Gargoyles, united in purpose and strength, filled the cavernous space, their numbers dwarfing the population of any village she'd ever known. The sight infused her with newfound courage, bolstering her wavering faith.

"Besides," added Drygor, "I'm confident that the imprisoned gargoyles will join our fight for freedom. We won't be alone in this battle."

His reassurance washed over Strymar like a warm wave, easing her fears and solidifying her conviction.

"I've just had a thought," said a younger male gargoyle. "What about the abandoned villages? Do you think any still stand?"

Drygor stroked his chin thoughtfully, considering the question.

"The village where I lived isn't far from here," he mused. "But whether it's still standing... that's hard to say."

"I'm sorry to tell you this," said Strymar, her

expression clouded with disappointment, "but if the humans haven't taken it over, they've surely burnt it to the ground."

"We'll make them pay," Drygor said with a growl, his voice a low rumble of raw fury. "For every home destroyed and every life shattered, the humans will be made to answer to us."

Chapter Twelve

Strymar stared at the chalk map drawn on the stone floor, her features etched with concentration. The crude lines and shapes were a weak representation of the treacherous terrain above ground, but it was still the best map they had, despite its limitations. Around her, the strategy team spoke amongst themselves. Deep in thought, she had almost managed to tune them out entirely.

"Is there something troubling you?" Drygor asked, his gravelly voice gentle.

Strymar glanced at him, noting the concern on his battle-scarred face.

"I'm just thinking back to my encounter with that human from the Inner Circle," she said. "In my urgency to escape, I had no chance to pick up vital information. I have no idea where the Inner Circle are based or how big their population is. Are they just as dangerous as the Opal Faction? Do they have a prison for gargoyles too, or do they simply kill them straight away?"

"Easy, Strymar," Drygor said, his tone comforting. "We can only work with what we know. We'll figure out the rest once we've gained ground from the Opal Faction. A lack of information is always less than ideal, but it's not insurmountable."

The strategy team members nodded in agreement, their expressions resolute.

"With all the training and preparations we're committed to," Drygor continued, "and with the gargoyles we aim to free from the prison on our side, I believe we can face the Inner Circle once we find out where they're hiding."

"That reminds me," Strymar said, her voice passionate, her words punctuated by memories of her own imprisonment. "During my escape, when I got to the lake, I could barely fly. I wasn't sure that I'd make it. I was hungry, thirsty, and wounded. We need to make sure we've got plenty of food, water and medical supplies. It is inevitable that some of the prisoners will have no chance without them."

"Agreed," said Drygor, making a mental note of the supplies they'd need. "I'll instruct our soldiers to be prepared to carry the weaker ones if necessary."

"Some gargoyles will definitely need more help than others," Strymar confirmed, her tone laced with sadness. "Some of the gargoyles will be frail – not just on account of old age, but from the awful conditions they've been living in for so long."

"Is the lake the only part of the journey that will require flight?" Drygor asked.

"Yes," Strymar answered. "For all other terrain, it's essential that we don't fly unless we absolutely have to. Although the Opal Faction have hounds to chase us down on foot, they have bows and arrows to shoot us with in the event that we become airborne."

As the strategy team absorbed this information, Drygor shifted their focus once more.

"Now, let's discuss the layout of the prison itself," he asserted. "We need to ensure that no gargoyle is left behind, and that none of our soldiers risk getting lost in the maze of cells and corridors."

Strymar took a deep breath, recalling her time imprisoned within those walls.

"This very lair has probably prepared you all for the type of navigating you'll need to do once we're inside the prison," she said. "There are hundreds of cramped cells, along with corridors and an exercise yard."

She hesitated, her eyes darkening with the memories of blood and death.

"Go on," Drygor said, patient yet encouraging.

"There's no easy way to say this," Strymar said, sighing as she carefully chose her words. "Everyone needs to prepare themselves for the likelihood that once inside the prison, they'll come across the bodies of dead gargoyles. It's not uncommon for the guards to leave a gargoyle in the spot where they perished – it breaks the morale of the prisoners, and hell, do they know it! It will be difficult, but we must remain strong-willed and unshakable in the face of such horror."

Drygor nodded solemnly, appreciative of Strymar's insight.

"We've seen death before in our leadership challenges," he said, his voice heavy with emotion. "But the deaths of our imprisoned kin are different. They had no choice, no chance at a fair fight and a dignified end. We must remember that – as we fight for their freedom, and for our own."

As Drygor made a mental note to share essential information with the gargoyles who would be fighting on the front line, the strategy team members exchanged grim nods, each steeling themselves for the challenges ahead.

With a piece of chalk in his grip, one of the strategy team members crouched down on the stone floor, carefully drawing the layout of the prison as Strymar described it in more detail. The sound of their fellow gargoyles training in the background provided a constant reminder of what was at stake.

"Is this accurate?" the gargoyle asked, looking up at Strymar as he sketched the last corridor.

Strymar peered at the map, her face a picture of concentration.

"Yes," she confirmed, nodding slowly. "That looks right – just so long as everyone is mindful that there may be parts of the prison I've never seen before."

"Don't worry about that," Drygor assured. "Once our army has infiltrated the known areas of the prison, we'll leave nowhere unchecked. We'll find and kill every last one of those bastard guards who have tortured and killed our kind."

Strymar's eyes flashed with determination, mirroring Drygor's resolve. She knew that the upcoming battle would be brutal, but essential. As the strategy team continued their discussion, refining their plans, she couldn't help but think of her fellow prisoners, still trapped in that hellish place.

The grunts of exertion from the training area intermingled with her memories of captivity. Even now, the stench of blood and fear seemed to linger in her nostrils, a constant reminder of the horrors she had witnessed. She shook her head vigorously, refusing to let the flashbacks paralyse her. Instead, she would channel her pain and use it to fuel her motivation.

As she looked around at the faces of the gargoyles nearest to her, a fire burned in their eyes – a flame of vengeance that would soon be unleashed upon their enemies. Though Strymar knew that the road ahead would be treacherous, she took comfort in the knowledge that she was not alone. Together, the gargoyles would rise from the shadows, and the world above would tremble at their wrath.

Chapter Thirteen

The main hall of the underground lair was alive with anticipation, a palpable energy buzzing through the air. Gargoyles of all shapes and sizes filled the cavernous space, their armoured bodies casting jagged shadows on the rough stone walls. Grydovyn stood tall on a raised plinth, his wise eyes surveying the assembled warriors.

"My fellow gargoyles," he began, his voice echoing throughout the hall. "For three days, we have trained, forged weapons, and laid plans. Now, we are ready to fight."

He paused, allowing the gravity of his words to sink in. The gargoyles listened raptly, hearts beating faster, and wings twitching nervously.

"Each of you has shown great dedication and skill during our training. I am proud to call you my comrades in arms."

Heads lifted and chests swelled with pride. Everyone beamed at their own small but vital contribution. Grydovyn's gaze swept over them all, each warrior basking in the feeling of his approval.

"Remember that in the heat of battle, you are not alone," he said, his voice ringing with conviction. "We stand together, united by a common goal: to free our brethren and strike a blow against those who would see us eradicated. Believe in yourselves, as I do, and know that your strength lies within."

A chorus of roars erupted from the crowd, a cacophony of determination and defiance. For generations, they had dwelt in the shadows, hidden from the cruel human world above. Now, they were poised to make their stand, to fight for their freedom and restore their dignity.

Grydovyn raised his arm for silence, causing the hall to quieten once more.

"Take up your weapons, my friends, and let us march forth. For tonight, we bring the fight to the Opal Faction. Tonight, we take back our freedom!"

The gargoyles surged forward, snatching up

their freshly-forged weapons and securing them to their armour. The air crackled with enthusiasm as they readied themselves for the journey ahead. There was no time for hesitation or doubt. They had trained, prepared, and now it was time to act. It was time to make the Opal Faction pay for their crimes against gargoylekind.

With Grydovyn and Drygor leading from the front, the warriors filed out of the hall. As they marched forward through the winding tunnels of their subterranean home, their collective resolve only grew stronger. The atmosphere was charged with a stoic vigour, a thunderous energy that filled the air as though it were a living force.

"By the ancients, I can't believe we're finally doing this," whispered one young gargoyle to another, his voice trembling with a mixture of excitement and fear.

"It's about time we showed those humans what we're capable of," said another, tightly gripping the hilt of her sword.

"Stay close and follow my lead," Drygor barked out.

The warriors marched through the labyrinthine passages like a well-oiled machine, the sound of their unified footsteps vibrating against the ancient walls.

Within the inside of the large tree trunk, the dedicated gargoyles unfurled their wings like silent banners of intent. As one, they synchronised their movements in flight, creating a rhythmic symphony as they propelled themselves upwards. The echoes of their effort – in wingbeats and from the scrape of claws against bark – resonated within each warrior like a primal heartbeat.

Finally, the front of the procession emerged from the lair's threshold and into the moonlit night, the scent of moss and aged wood stark and distinctive. As more gargoyles emerged to find themselves no longer underground, many looked back in amazement at the entrance to their lair. It had been so long since they had seen the outside of the enormous tree trunk, its gnarled roots and thick foliage providing a natural camouflage.

For many, this was their first glimpse of the outside world in decades. The sight was both awe-inspiring and terrifying. For some, the rich blend of unfamiliar sensations was almost overwhelming – the cool, crisp air against their skin; the scent of damp earth and verdant foliage; the hushed rustling of leaves as nocturnal creatures stirred in the darkness.

"It's been so long," muttered one gargoyle, his voice thick with emotion. "I'd almost forgotten what it feels like."

"Enjoy it while you can," cautioned another, her eyes darting nervously through the shadows. "We've got a long journey ahead of us, and the humans won't take kindly to our presence."

"By the gods," murmured an older gargoyle, staring up at the vast expanse of sky. "I'd forgotten how beautiful it is up here."

"Beautiful, but dangerous," warned Grydovyn, scanning the surrounding area for any signs of danger. "Keep your wits about you, my friends. We must move swiftly and silently from now on."

"Exactly," Drygor said in a loud whisper, his gravelly voice cutting through everyone's lingering awe. "The time for marvelling is over. We have a mission to complete."

He then turned to Strymar, his expression one

of respect and admiration.

"I want you at the front, Strymar," he instructed. "Lead us through this unfamiliar world. Take us to the Opal Faction's prison. We need your expertise now more than ever."

***

With Strymar at the helm, the gargoyles soon arrived at the large lake.

"Remember, keep low and quiet," Drygor reminded them. "We don't want to alert the humans to our presence."

With expert precision, the gargoyles glided over the lake, their claws skimming the water's surface, sending ripples in their wake. Each one felt the weight of their mission pressing upon them, making their hearts beat faster and their wings work harder.

Upon reaching the other side of the lake, everyone then entered the wooded area that lay beyond.

"Stay close and watch your footing," Drygor instructed, quiet but urgent. "This terrain is treacherous."

Beneath the mosaic of towering trees, the gargoyles moved with a quiet grace, their forms seamlessly blending with the shadows of the wooded realm. Silhouettes against the shifting tapestry of foliage, they advanced in disciplined unity, wings tightly folded in a collective vow of silence. Each footfall, a muted vibration on the leaf-strewn ground, resonated with the subtlety of the breeze rustling through the branches. As they traversed the seasoned expanse, they navigated with an instinctive awareness, adapting their movements to the natural rhythm of the environment.

As they left the cover of the woods, the scent of humans – like rotten meat and stale sweat – grew stronger. Entering a barren landscape dotted with horses, carts, and stables, the once-hidden gargoyles were now exposed, their forms standing out against the moonlit ground.

"Move quickly and quietly," ordered Drygor, his voice barely above a whisper. "We can't afford to be spotted now."

The gargoyles did as commanded, skilfully slinking through the open space, adrenaline coursing through their veins as the prison loomed ever closer.

Chapter Fourteen

"Stay sharp, everyone," Drygor muttered assertively, his eyes scanning the horizon for any sign of danger. "Our moment is almost upon us."

The prison loomed before the gargoyle soldiers, a monolith of cold stone and iron that stood like a cruel sentinel amid the desolate landscape. Its walls were tall, imposing, and crowned with razor-sharp spikes – a silent warning to those who dared approach. The gargoyles stared at the fortress, a chilling realisation settling into the pits of their stomachs.

"Keep it together, everyone," Drygor whispered through gritted teeth, his eyes never leaving the prison. "We've made it this far. We just need to find a way in."

Strymar could feel her heart hammering in her chest, her body tense with the anticipation of battle. She scanned the walls, her mind racing as she searched for any sign of weakness. When she spotted a particularly compromised spot in the structure, she brought it to Drygor's attention with an urgent gesture.

"Everyone! There!" Drygor whispered, pointing to a shadowy crevice near the base of the wall. "You see that crack down there: if we chip away at it, strategically, quickly, and as quietly as we can, we should be able to create a gap just big enough for us to slip through one by one."

In unison, the gargoyles brandished their weapons – sharpened claws and honed blades that gleamed in the muted moonlight. The weapons, wielded with delicate precision, found purchase in the crevices of the stone wall. Everyone worked in tandem, applying measured force in order to gradually increase the gap. The metallic vibrato of their efforts harmonised with the still of the night in a symphony of stealth.

Drygor, vigilant for any sign of detection, observed as the gap widened, inch by inch. Every gargoyle, with an acute awareness of the need for both speed and discretion, contributed to the collective effort that would soon breach the barrier of captivity.

As soon as the gap was big enough, the legion prepared for the orchestrated entry. Grydovyn, with a nod that conveyed readiness, signalled for the first gargoyle to slip through. The shadows enveloped the army like a protective cloak as they infiltrated the prison one by one, a silent procession of rebellion.

The gargoyles squeezed their way through the narrow alcove, twisting and contorting to fit through the tight space. It was an uncomfortable, claustrophobic process, but they knew there was no other way of entering the prison. As she moved along, Strymar's thoughts were consumed by memories of her own imprisonment and escape. The stench of fear and despair clung to the air, a putrid miasma that churned her stomach and tightened her throat.

"Alright," Drygor whispered as the last soldier emerged from the tunnel. "We're in. Let's move."

The gargoyles crept through the prison's dark corridors, shadows flickering across their faces as they moved with silent determination. Every creak and each distant patter of footsteps made them pause, breaths held and muscles tensed in anticipation of an attack that never came.

"This place is a maze," a young gargoyle muttered under his breath, his wings twitching with agitation.

"Keep moving," Drygor whispered urgently, his eyes flitting between the countless corridors branching off before them. "We'll find the cells soon enough."

"Wait," Grydovyn murmured, holding up a gnarled claw for silence.

He cocked his head to the side, listening intently to the faint sounds of conversation drifting down the hall.

"Guards," he mouthed. "Just around the corner."

Strymar listened to the voices of the human guards. She could also hear the ragged breaths and soft whimpers of the gargoyle prisoners, a testament to the cruelty they had endured at the hands of their captors. Despite the rage that boiled within, she forced herself to stay focused; her sole objective now was to save every last prisoner.

Drygor issued the signal informing all to prepare for the imminent assault. A few moments later, he communicated the silent cue to proceed, seamlessly guiding everyone into action. Raring to go, the gargoyle soldiers sprang forward from the shadows with the precision of a well-choreographed dance.

In the blink of an eye, the corridor became a battleground as the gargoyle army engaged the unsuspecting guards in a flurry of calculated strikes. Contrasting against the swift and silent efficiency of the ambush, the clash of metal against metal rang out in the dank air.

Gargoyles, with wings unfurled and with glares of predatory focus, outmanoeuvred the guards in the confined space, the tide of the skirmish in their favour.

One guard, disarmed by a swift stroke of a gargoyle's claws, relinquished a jingling set of keys. Drygor, recognising the crucial opportunity, swiftly retrieved the keys and nodded in silent approval. The confrontation, as quickly as it had erupted, subsided into the muted annals of gargoyle victory.

With the stolen keys in their possession, the gargoyles now had the means to unlock the prison cells that held their captive kin. The dark corridors, witness to the clandestine dance of liberation, became the silent stage upon which the gargoyle soldiers continued their journey deeper into the heart of the prison.

"It's not over yet," Drygor bellowed, his voice impassioned. "We mustn't let a single guard walk free. We mustn't leave anyone behind."

In the sprawling maze of the prison's confines, the gargoyle army moved with a purpose that echoed in the hallowed corridors. Drygor directed the legion through the shadowed recesses where each step held the weight of liberation. The air, thick with the scent of iron and confinement, became a battlefield where freedom clashed against the oppressive grip of captivity.

As they advanced, the gargoyle army encountered many clusters of human guards, each confrontation unfolding in a flurry of violence. Yet, for every captive gargoyle set free, the cost manifested in the agony of fallen comrades, the darkness absorbing the hollow lament of loss in the name of liberation.

Some of the liberated prisoners, though emaciated and worn, lent their strength to the gargoyle cause. Wielding weapons taken from the human guards, their long-silenced voices found resonance in the collective chorus of defiance.

Amidst the unity, there were those among the freed prisoners who bore the impact of captivity more acutely. Starved and weakened, their skeletal frames carried the visible toll of their torment. In an act of camaraderie, gargoyle soldiers protected the feeble among them, their wings shielding those too affected by hunger and pain, enabling them to traverse the prison's unforgiving terrain.

"We have left no stone unturned," Grydovyn announced. "We have stormed every part of the prison, and now all guards have been slain."

"Let's get everyone out of here," Drygor commanded, his gaze falling on the freed prisoners, some trembling with exhaustion, others fighting back tears. "We'll tend to the wounded and make sure everyone's accounted for. Then we move."

With adrenaline still pumping through their veins, the gargoyles moved with haste as they administered vital aid and comfort to those in need. As the reality of their victory began to sink in, they shared embraces and profound words of acknowledgement, all whilst refusing to forget the sacrifices made.

"Alright, everyone," Drygor called out, his voice carrying through the now liberated prison. "Let's get out of here, and never look back."

Epilogue

Emerging from the prison's shadowed grasp, the assembly of gargoyle soldiers and liberated prisoners embarked on the journey back to the underground lair.

The air, thick with the elation of newfound freedom, carried the ripples of a collective exhale – a respite earned in the crucible of defiance. However, a sense of urgency lingered in every rustle of leaves and with every scrape of claws against the earth, for everyone remained aware that the gloom beyond harboured the unseen eyes of potential adversaries; the slain prison guards were but a fraction of the human population that lived in nearby villages beyond the woods.

As the night unfurled its canvas, the gargoyle army pressed forward, driven by the unyielding desire to return to the underground lair before the impending dawn. The urgency heightened as the moon sailed across the night sky, a celestial timekeeper marking the precious moments before sunrise.

When the gargoyle army arrived safely beyond the entrance of their underground lair, the guards stationed at the threshold could hardly believe their eyes. Their expressions reflected the shared anxiety of those who had remained behind to wait in eager anticipation.

Only the echoes of footsteps against the stone floor announced the return of the warriors. As news of the triumphant liberation spread, excited chatter pooled through the chamber. A mosaic of relief, happiness, and unspoken gratitude painted the faces of those who had kept the home fires burning.

With everyone gathered in the heart of the lair's grand chamber, wings unfurled in joyous gestures of greeting. Loved ones embraced, eyes gleaming with tears of relief as the returning soldiers were enveloped in a sea of familial recognition. On the outskirts of the chamber, makeshift medical stations had been prepared in advance. Skilled guards hastily set to work grinding medicinal herbs, and dressing wounds. Wings were examined with precision, and claws were tended to with meticulous care. The warmth of communal relief became a sanctuary for all gargoyles who had weathered the storm. Those whose loved ones didn't make it back to the lair were offered an abundance of sympathy and support.

Despite the euphoric feeling of victory, a collective understanding hung in the air that the liberation of gargoyles from the Opal Faction's prison marked only the start of what would be a long and challenging war. It would rage on not only against the Opal Faction, but the Inner Circle too.

The shared grasp of the challenges ahead would serve to nourish the gargoyle community as a united force – and one to be reckoned with. Together, they would remain committed to their cause, fighting on passionately, striving to see the day when the skies could bear witness to the triumphant return of gargoyles flying free – without fear of capture, and without fear of imprisonment, torture, and death.

Although the war ahead would not be simple and would certainly come with sacrifices, the first step had been taken. The future, though veiled in uncertainty, glimmered with the possibilities of reclamation and renewal.

130